The
WITCHES
of
BENEVENTO

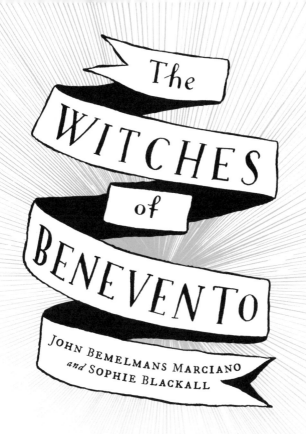

The WITCHES of BENEVENTO

JOHN BEMELMANS MARCIANO
and SOPHIE BLACKALL

BEWARE THE CLOPPER!

A Maria Beppina Story

VIKING

VIKING

An imprint of Penguin Random House LLC

375 Hudson Street

New York, New York 10014

First published in the United States of America by Viking,
an imprint of Penguin Random House LLC, 2016

Text copyright © 2016 by John Bemelmans Marciano

Illustrations copyright © 2016 by Sophie Blackall

LIBRARY OF CONGRESS CATALOGING-IN-PUBLICATION DATA IS AVAILABLE.

ISBN: 9780451471826

1 3 5 7 9 10 8 6 4 2

Manufactured in China   Set in IM FELL French Canon
Book design by Nancy Brennan

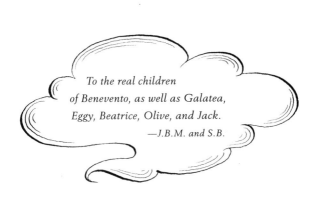

To the real children
of Benevento, as well as Galatea,
Eggy, Beatrice, Olive, and Jack.
—J.B.M. and S.B.

Emilio

Rosa

Primo

Maria Beppina

Sergio

CONTENTS

They say that there are no curious children in Benevento. There can't be, for a curious child would never last long here.

In Benevento, danger lurks at every turn, from mischiefing Janara to grabby Manalonga, from evil spirits who lurk in archways to demons—such as myself and my friends here—who hide in animal form.

And then . . . there's the CLOPPER!

The Clopper lurks in the remains of the ancient Roman Theater, chasing children who dare to cross it. Some say she's a Janara trapped outside of her body, others that she is a goddess whose powers have fizzled, and still others that she's an old lady made crazy by the loss of her baby countless moons ago. (I know the truth, but I'll never tell!)

To avoid the many dangers of Benevento, children must learn to say their spells, make the correct offerings, and know when to RUN. Just as you won't get hit if you look both ways before crossing the street, witches shouldn't bother you so long as you follow the rules.

But . . . what happens when the rules start to change? Or you can't run fast enough? Or—most **dangerous** of all— you start to get CURIOUS.

YOUR CONSTANT FRIEND,
SIGISMONDO
(WITH BRUNO AND RAFAELLA)

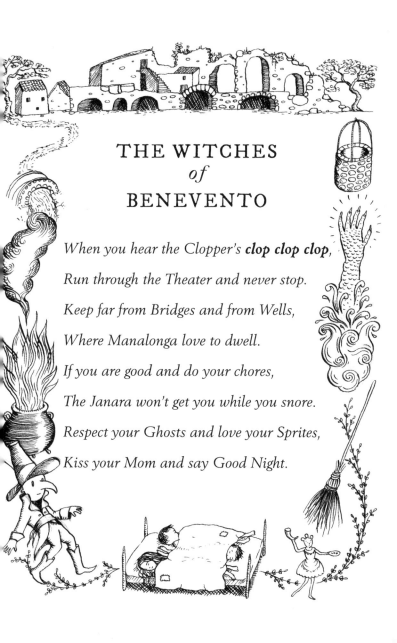

THE WITCHES
of
BENEVENTO

*When you hear the Clopper's **clop clop clop**,*

Run through the Theater and never stop.

Keep far from Bridges and from Wells,

Where Manalonga love to dwell.

If you are good and do your chores,

The Janara won't get you while you snore.

Respect your Ghosts and love your Sprites,

Kiss your Mom and say Good Night.

BEWARE THE CLOPPER!

A Maria Beppina Story

1

TOO SLOW

"ARE you guys ready?" Primo says.

Right now, all the kids are at the edge of the open courtyard of the Theater, bracing themselves for a race with the Clopper. Maria Beppina has a lump in her throat.

This is the worst part of her day.

Maria Beppina is *always* the last kid to make it through the Theater. She is the slowest kid in the Triggio, and she's afraid that one day the Clopper is going to get her.

None of the other witches in town bother Maria Beppina. The reason is that she is excellent at following rules.

Maria Beppina always keeps to the middle of bridges and sings *LA-la-la-la-LA!* at the top of her lungs, and never once has she heard the voice of a Manalonga. She hangs salt on her door every night, even though Janara rarely do mischiefs inside the town walls. She not only gives the horns and spits when she walks through the arch but holds her breath too, lest she inhale any bad magic from Malefix, the nasty spirit who lives there.

The problem with the Clopper is that avoiding her has nothing to do with following rules. It is a test of physical ability. And when it comes to stuff like that, Maria Beppina isn't excellent at all.

"Let's do it!" Primo shouts, and all the kids take off racing, giggling and laughing as they go. Already, Maria Beppina is behind.

Her dad doesn't believe that witches exist. He thinks to get by in life you just need to read books and be smart. He doesn't understand that sometimes you have to be strong. Or fast.

The other kids are getting farther and farther ahead. Maria Beppina feels like she is almost caught.

clop clop clop!

Not only is the sound of the one wooden shoe of the witch getting louder—she can feel the Clopper's breath on her neck!

Maria Beppina can see that Rosa is already to the other side. Primo is just a couple of steps behind her, like always. But now Emilio and Sergio are across too, and she's still running.

"Come on, Maria Beppina!" Sergio yells.

ClopclopclopCLOPCLOPCLOP!

Finally, Maria Beppina makes it to the safety of the other side. It is like waking from a nightmare to realize you are safe in bed. She feels a stitch in her side like a needle in her ribs. All the kids are huffing and puffing, hands on their knees. Well, all the kids except Rosa.

"If you don't watch out," Primo says to Maria Beppina, "the Clopper's gonna get you!"

"What would—*huff huff*—happen if—*huff huff*—she did?" Maria Beppina says.

Everybody laughs. "Nobody's *ever* been caught by the Clopper!" Primo says, mocking her.

"It's true," Emilio agrees, as a point of fact.

Maria Beppina would blush, but her face is

already so red from running it can't get redder.

"But what *would* happen?" Sergio says. "Would she strangle you? Would she drag you down to the Underworld like a Manalonga and turn you into her servant? Would she roast you on a spit and eat you?"

No one knows, not even Emilio. And no one wants to find out, either.

Maria Beppina, however, can't sleep all night. This isn't because of the mischiefs of any Janara, but from something even more unsettling: curiosity.

ACHO

2
LIFE WITH DADDY

*THE Metamorphoses . . . Orlando Furioso . . .
The Odyssey . . .*

Maria Beppina puts down the feather
duster and sneezes. Her father says, "*Salute,*"
which means "health."

"Daddy, do we really need to dust all these
books?"

"I think your sneeze answers that question," Daddy says, not looking up from the map
he is working on.

What she really wants to say is, *Daddy, do
we really need all these books?* It makes everyone in the Triggio think they're weird. None
of Maria Beppina's friends even know how to

read, and not their parents either. Bad enough that her father surveys land and draws maps, and even worse that he's from Naples. It makes them like foreigners here.

Maria Beppina opens a shutter, and immediately gets carried away on the smell of the air. It's such a beautiful day outside! Not a cloud in the sky.

"Close that shutter!" Daddy says. "I don't want the wind blowing my papers around."

"There's no breeze," Maria Beppina says under her breath as she closes the window. She then cracks it back open quietly, just a bit.

She wishes she could be outdoors like her friends. Maria Beppina under-stands that she has to do the household chores—there are only the two of them, after all—but to also have to do reading and math and history lessons, it's not fair! Her friends and cousins all work, but doing fun things. Outside things.

Today could have been different. Today the Twins asked her to help on the farm. *All* the kids went to help, and *all* the parents let them. Except hers.

For days, the Janara have been doing mischiefs at the Twins'—everyone is talking about it—but today's was the worst. All the tiles got blown off the barn roof last night and scattered into the fields.

It's crazy! Janara never go that far. But what's *really* unsettling is that it's too early for Mischief Season. And it isn't *just* at the Twins' farm, either—it's all across the countryside.

Maria Beppina doesn't like it, not one bit. There are rules that even witches are supposed to live by. If the rules aren't followed, how can anyone ever feel safe?

"Can I please go now?" Maria Beppina says. "I finished everything."

"Yes, yes, you can go," Daddy says, still not looking up.

Maria Beppina opens the door and feels several large, fat drops of rain fall on her. By the time she gets to the bottom of the stairs she has to run right back up—it's a storm. How is that possible? It was the perfect day just a minute ago!

"The window!" Daddy says, holding his papers down as his eye-glasses fall off his nose.

"The blasted window! When I tell you to shut it I mean *lock* it!"

Maria Beppina closes the wind-blown shutters, getting her face drenched in the process. She's disappointed at not getting to go to the Twins', but also worried. Does this sudden storm have anything to do with the early Mischief Season? And when the Clopper almost caught her the other day, was that part of it too?

"Don't you think it's strange," she says, "that the weather would change all at once?"

"It's spring," Daddy says. "That's what happens in spring."

"People say that when the weather changes like this it's because of Janara."

Daddy drops his compass and finally looks up from his map. "How many times have I told you not to *listen* to that nonsense! Witches don't exist! That everyone here believes in them only goes to show how small-minded and superstitious and *stupid* the people who live in this town are."

"But how can you deny it?" Maria Beppina says. "The farmers are all going crazy with the mischiefs—they say it's the worst Janara Season ever! And Sergio has a ghost living upstairs that he has to spend half the day taking care of!"

"Have you ever seen this ghost?"

"Well, no," Maria Beppina says. "Only *he* can."

"Sergio." Her dad shakes his head, looking in the direction of his house, right across the alley. "That is one strange boy. . . ."

"Well, I hear the clopping of the Clopper every time I run through the Theater," Maria Beppina says. "The other day she almost caught me!"

"You know who built that theater, don't you?"

Maria Beppina groans inside, because she knows what's coming next. The Romans.

"The *Romans* built that theater! Almost two thousand years ago, and look at it! Still standing." Daddy raises a triumphant finger in the air. "That's engineering! That's Science!"

"How can you know everything the Romans did two thousand years ago," Maria Beppina says, "but have *no* idea what's happening to the people around you right here, right now?"

"Trust me, Maria Beppina. There is *nothing* that happens that cannot be explained by Science."

"But even *you* think that the rooster who belongs to the blacksmith is a demon."

"Now that *is* true," her dad says. "That blasted rooster! He jumped on my shoulder and practically pecked a hole in my head yesterday. I can hardly go outside!"

Maria Beppina is about to ask her father how Science can explain a demon taking the form of a rooster, but she never gets the chance.

3

A BAD OMEN

TOC TOC

Maria Beppina knows that knock. It's Primo. She opens the door to her cousin standing there, getting soaked in the pouring rain.

"Dinner," he says. "Eel."

"Hey, Primo, how was . . ." She was going to finish the sentence ". . . *putting the roof back on the Twins' barn?*" but her cousin is already splashing his way back downstairs.

Maria Beppina feels her face burn. She and her dad live upstairs from her cousins. On the one hand, it's great, because Maria Beppina gets to be a part of their family. On the other hand, she's *not* a part of their family—not totally.

Maria Beppina sneaks away without her dad noticing she's barefoot (she's the *only* kid who has to wear shoes) and rushes down the stairs into the driving, deafening rain. She fast opens the door to her cousins' and—

"**NO!**" Primo's entire family yells.

She feels something slimy pass over her bare foot. It is the grossest, *yuckiest* feeling she has ever had to feel. Maria Beppina looks down and sees a fat black eel, its tail now slithering over her toes and the rest of it out the door.

The next moment, Primo is pushing past her, and she slips and falls against the door to the ground, tripping Isidora and holding up the rest of the family.

"Get out of the way! Dinner is on the loose!"

Butt soaked, Maria Beppina gets herself up, and does her best to race after everyone, but even Primo's grandmother is faster than she is.

Maria Beppina feels dumb and embarrassed. *Please, oh please, let Primo catch that eel!*

But he doesn't.

The eel swims through the flooded streets all the way to the Cemetery of Dead Babies. Maria Beppina can't see what's going on, but she hears Primo's family all yelling at him, "Go get it!"

He waits too long and the eel slithers down the well in front of the cemetery chapel.

Everyone turns on each other—Aunt Zufia

blames Uncle Mimì, Uncle
Mimì blames Aunt Zufia,
Isidora blames Primo—but
all Maria Beppina hears is Primo
blame *her* for opening the door.

They all start back toward home, and Maria
Beppina is glad at least for the rain, so no one
can see her tears.

4

A SHORT CHAPTER WHICH LEAVES EVERYONE HUNGRY

DINNER is slim pickings. The kids scour the bottom of the pasta barrel for every last broken strand of spaghetti, and dream about the eel meal that could have been. Gloomying the mood further is Primo's momma, who is still mad at his poppa. Uncle Mimì, however, is never gloomy.

"So long as I have my *maccheroni,* I am a happy man," Uncle Mimì says, holding some long, stringy noodles above his mouth and slurping them down. "No king could be happier!"

"Why did you bother getting the eel, then?" Aunt Zufia grumbles.

"Momma, can I have *more?*" Primo says.

"There is no more!"

"What about *that* plate?" he says, pointing.

"That's for your uncle," Aunt Zufia says, meaning Maria Beppina's dad. "You can have bread if you're still hungry."

"But it's as hard as a rock!" Primo says.

"Then soak it in some water."

Primo makes a face and cleans his plate with a finger.

Primo's sister Isidora starts clearing the table, and Maria Beppina helps her. In the meantime, Nonna Jovanna keeps talking about what just happened.

"Forget your hunger! That eel! That eel is the worst sign I have ever *seen*!" she says, gripping the red-chili-pepper charm on her necklace. It wards off the evil spirits that might be angry at her for talking about this. "A fish that swims in the streets! What will it be next? Manalonga in the trees?"

Maria Beppina's aunt and uncle just roll

their eyes whenever Nonna Jovanna gets like this. They believe in witches of course—only her dad doesn't—but Nonna Jovanna is always finding the worst signs in anything that is the least bit out of the ordinary. But still, there's something about her bug-eyed gaze tonight that spooks Maria Beppina.

Primo brings a bunch of dishes to the tub to wash. He *never* does that.

"*Psst!*" he whispers to Maria Beppina. "I have to tell you something!"

"What is it?" she whispers back.

"I saw a Manalonga!" he says. "In the well. *That's* why I didn't grab the eel. It was talking to me. It even reached up to grab me!" He drops the plates in with a *clink* and a splash. "I'm almost sure it did!"

"Here, Maria Beppina," Aunt Zufia says, handing her the plate with the last few strands of *maccheroni* on it. "Bring this up to your father."

The rain has broken into a drizzle, which Maria Beppina doesn't mind. What she *does* mind is that something strange is going on. Nonna Jovanna was right about the eel being a bad sign. It was *leading* Primo to a Manalonga! Just the thought of it gives Maria Beppina goosebumps.

If only her father were right, about there being no such thing as witches.

But he's not.

5

LAUNDRY DAY

TOC TOC

Maria Beppina is just finishing putting the laundry into a sack when she hears Primo's knock.

"Hey, cousin!" Primo says, sounding unusually happy to see Maria Beppina.

He walks right past her to Daddy's stacks of books. "So, what do you know about *augurs*?" he says, staring at the books like a flock of strange birds he's never seen before.

"I've heard my dad talk about them," she says. "How Roman priests would read the insides of animals and stuff." *Skeevo*, she thinks.

"You know all the weird things that have been going on? Well, I bet we can figure out why it's all happening if we augur an animal or two." Primo points at the stacks. "Do you think your dad has a *book* about it?"

"Let's see," she says, coming over to look. She wants to help, especially if her knowing how to read can for once be something useful rather than freakish. "He has lots of stuff about the Romans. He loves the Romans."

"You can really read all that?" Primo says skeptically, pointing at the titles on the spines.

"Pretty much," Maria Beppina says, feeling proud.

But she can't find any books about augurs, or Roman religion, or anything like that. "Daddy says these encyclopedias are the best, but they're in French."

"So?"

"I don't know French."

"Oh," Primo says, nodding. "So you *can't* really read."

"Well, not *every* language!" she says. "But here, there's got to be something in one of these." She pulls out a different encyclopedia and looks up *Augur.*

"*In ancient Rome,*" Maria Beppina begins, "*augers were priests who read the will of the gods through natural phenomena.*"

"Come on, come on," Primo says after a few more paragraphs like that. "Get to the good part! How do you *do* it? Like split the stomach open and stuff."

Maria Beppina begins to skim. It turns out that auguring is about a lot more than innards. Anything can be a sign. "There's something about lightning moving from left to right bringing good fortune," she says hopefully. "And that it's bad luck to meet a raven when you go outside."

"But what about the animal guts?"

"Oh wait, here's something," she says. "*The main way to discover the will of the gods was to examine the organs of animals killed for sacrifice. Priests believed that anything peculiar should be taken as a warning.*"

"Anything peculiar?" he says. "Like what kind of peculiar?"

"So *this* is where you've been!" comes a voice from outside.

Isidora pushes through the partly open door. "Come on, you lazy toad," she says to Primo. "We have to do the washing. And *no* getting out of it this time!"

As Primo rolls his eyes, Isidora shoves the basket of laundry she's carrying into his gut. "*Oof!*" he says. "Hey, watch it!"

Isidora sees Maria Beppina's sack of laundry and tells her to come along too. Maria Beppina hems and haws but follows. The reason for the hemming/hawing is the Theater, which they will arrive at soon.

As in now.

Maria Beppina clutches at her lumpy bag of dirty things and feels her heart race, looking across her field of fears.

She has been taking the long way around the Theater ever since the Clopper almost caught her, walking along the city walls or taking one of the far gates out of town. She's not sure she can make it across, especially with this big heavy sack. But she can't act like a coward in front of her downstairs cousins, who are off and running! She takes off too.

clop clop clop clop clop clop clop clop clop!

How can the Clopper already be so close? Maria Beppina feels her shoes too loose, her heart thumping out of her chest, and clutches onto the bag like a pillow during a nightmare. And that's what it feels like—the mares at night, when they ride you, suffocating you, and you try to wake up and you can't and you can't and you can't.

CLOP CLOP CLOP!

When she does make it across, Maria Beppina can hardly believe it. She puts the laundry sack down so she can take full gulps of air. Primo and Isidora are already walking ahead, like it's nothing. Which to them, it is.

Maria Beppina follows her cousins down-stream to the wide shallow part of the river. Everyone does their washing here—it's far away from Manalonga, and the water is warmer. Except today it's *freezing*! Maria Beppina can barely stand it as she wades in.

She plucks a hair off her head—*ouch!*—and drops it into the water as an offering to Gallie, the kind spirit who lives in the river.

As the hair floats away, Maria Beppina sings:

Gallie, Gallie, Neptune's daughter,
Thank you for this lovely water.
A strand of hair I cast adrift.
Please take this, Gallie, as my gift.

Maria Beppina goes to where Primo, Rosa, and Emilio are standing near the far bank, arriving just as her cousin is telling the Twins about his scheme to augur an animal, specifically a fish. He insists he knows how to do it because of what he—or rather, *Maria Beppina*—read in a book.

"Isn't that right, Maria Beppina?" Primo says.

Now everyone is looking at her, and she can feel her face burn. Maria Beppina hates to lie, which is what it feels like Primo is asking her to do. She didn't read anything on how to *actually* augur an animal! Still, she doesn't want to disappoint her cousin.

"Well, we did read *about* auguring," Maria Beppina says, choosing her words carefully. "And it was *in* a book."

That seems to satisfy everyone, and Maria Beppina concentrates on washing while Primo and Rosa get to fishing.

She is nearly done when she sees Sergio arriving on the path from town. He can barely walk for the two sacks of laundry he's carrying. Leaving Primo and the Twins to augur and argue, Maria Beppina wades to the other bank of the river, where Sergio and 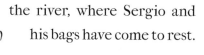 his bags have come to rest.

Maria Beppina has a secret—*very* secret—crush on Sergio. It must be said that Sergio is an unlikely person to have a crush on. He's a little funny looking, for one thing, with big gaps between his teeth and a sometimes squint in his eyes on account of his not seeing so well. But there is something cute about Sergio that makes you want to take care of him, like a puppy. Maria Beppina always wanted a puppy.

She sets her one small laundry bag down next to Sergio's two giant sacks. He is completely overwhelmed by what's inside of them: diapers. "How can three babies go caca this much?"

"Come on, I'll help you," Maria Beppina says.

She opens the first bag and catches a whiff that is so bad she starts breathing out of her mouth. Now her eyes start to water.

"It's not so bad," she says, forcing a smile.

While they wash, Maria Beppina talks about all that's been happening—like the eel and the Manalonga and how the Clopper is getting closer and closer to catching her. "And the Janara mischiefs are worse than ever at Rosa and Emilio's!"

"I don't understand why everyone's so worried about the Twins having a few days of Janara trouble," Sergio says. "I've had a whole *life* of ghost trouble!"

Sergio's ghost—whose name is Bis-Bis—demands two offerings a day, and they are a lot more involved than plucking a hair and saying a rhyme. If Sergio doesn't satisfy him, Bis-Bis will haunt the house and Sergio's family will have to move out.

Most of what Bis-Bis wants is food, but not only. "Today he wants me to get him rope," Sergio says. "What can a ghost *possibly* need with rope?!"

"Got one!" they hear Rosa yell from the far bank. She has a fish flapping on her spear, and Primo is hopping mad that she caught one first. Rosa always beats Primo at everything.

GOT ONE!

"I'll *never* finish all these diapers!" Sergio says, even though it's been Maria Beppina doing most of the work. "I can't believe my mom makes me do this!"

"Well, my dad wouldn't even let me go to the Twins' yesterday," Maria Beppina says. She wants to complain more about her father, but Sergio doesn't seem to hear her. When it comes to listening, he isn't much better than anyone else she knows.

"Hey, guys—come over and look at *this*!"

Primo is yelling and waving them across the river, where he and the Twins are huddled around something on the ground. It's the fish Rosa caught, lying cut open on the

muddy ground. But what Primo wants to show them is a ring. A *gold* ring.

"Where did you find it?" Sergio asks.

"There!" Primo says, and points to the gutted carp. "*Inside* the fish!"

At first, Maria Beppina thinks he's kidding. How could a ring—a beautiful gold ring—come from the inside of a fish? But it's true.

What was it that book said about auguring? **Anything peculiar should be taken as a warning.**

6

THE FIRE

THE next morning at Primo's stand, all the kids gather to hear what may be Primo's craziest scheme yet: He wants to go find the Tree of the Janara. Tonight!

Maria Beppina chokes at the thought of it. The Tree stands miles outside the city walls at the Bridge of Ancient Ages and is where witches gather before a night of mischiefing.

The reason Primo wants to go is the ring. He's convinced that the ring belongs to a Manalonga and so will protect them from Janara and demons. But how can he be sure?

"He's crazy!" Sergio says as they leave Primo at the stand.

"Do you think
we'll really find Janara?"
Maria Beppina asks on their way
down the hill. "And demons?"

She wonders if she might see the rooster
that attacks her dad. But how will she recog-
nize the rooster in its demon form? Will it still
have black feathers? A beak? Chicken feet?

"Forget Janara and demons!" Sergio says.
"Everyone knows **bandits** are what you really

need to be afraid
of outside the walls. I
heard that 'O Diavolino's band
hijacked the overnight coach from Naples
last week!"

"What do we have to worry about 'O
Diavolino for?" Emilio says. "We're not bringing any money, and we're not going to be anywhere near the highway. It's the bears and
wolves that might kill us."

"You're all a bunch of sissies! Wolves and
bears are nothing my trusty slingshot can't
handle," Rosa says, tapping her weapon. "And
as for Janara, they can't be too brave or they
wouldn't wait until everyone's asleep to go
sneaking around to do their mischiefs."

That afternoon, the kids who live inside the town walls—Maria Beppina, Sergio, and Primo—all tell their parents they are staying at the Twins', and vice versa.

At the end of dinner, Primo and Maria Beppina go and get Sergio, and the three of them meet up with the Twins on the mill path just outside the walls.

The walk is definitely long, but hardly scary at all. They even stop to make a nice big fire and have a snack in a clearing near a shepherd's hut.

When they arrive at the

Bridge of Ancient Ages, there are no Janara or demons and no tree that looks particularly supernatural.

Maria Beppina is relieved but feels bad for Primo, who is obviously disappointed and keeps insisting that they just got there too early and the Janara *will* come.

Sergio won't wait. He tells Primo he has to go home. "I can lie to my mother, but not my ghost," he says. "I can't miss the morning offering."

Maria Beppina says she has to go back too. "I'm sorry, Primo. I hope the Janara come!"

"Fine! *Quitters!* Who needs you anyway?" Primo calls after them.

Bad though she may feel for Primo, Maria Beppina feels a little rush of happiness to walk home alone with Sergio. But she soon feels a rush of a different kind—fear.

The two of them are *too* alone! Without Rosa and her slingshot, Primo and his confidence, and Emilio and his knowledge, it feels like they are going down a completely different path. The night has turned chilly, and Maria Beppina hugs herself as they walk.

They get into a patch of brambles that seems to go on and on. She doesn't remember having come through them the other way. And why haven't they come to the clearing where they made the fire?

"Are you sure we're going the right way?" Maria Beppina says.

"Sure I'm sure! We're following the river," Sergio says, pointing. "You can't lose a river!"

Except that you can and they have. The river narrows into a stream and peters out.

They somehow took a fork in the river.

"Dang!" Sergio says. "How far back the other way do we have to go?"

It is now *really* late, and every sound they hear is spookier and spookier. Maria Beppina can't decide what to worry about most—Janara, demons, bandits, or wild animals.

The two of them finally get back to where the stream meets the river and they turn down the path toward home.

Suddenly, they hear the sound of something breaking a stick. Loudly!

"Is it a wolf?" Sergio says.

"No, just a cat," Maria Beppina says as a tiger-striped puss dashes under a log.

"*Or* a demon," Sergio says, walking on. "Hey, what's that up ahead?"

Through the trees and underbrush they see a light. At first Maria Beppina wonders if it's from the moon. But it's not.

"It's a fire!" Sergio whispers, grabbing Maria Beppina's hand.

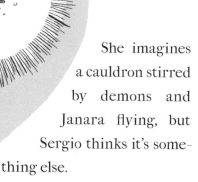

She imagines a cauldron stirred by demons and Janara flying, but Sergio thinks it's something else.

"Bandits!" he says. "We've stumbled onto a camp of *bandits*!"

Sergio squeezes Maria Beppina's hand tighter as they move forward. "I think I see one," Sergio says. "I think I see *three*! They're warming themselves by the fire."

They creep further toward the light, even though Maria Beppina isn't sure why they aren't running the other way.

At the edge of the clearing they hide behind a tree. But there are no bandits—at least none they can see. "But they *could* be in that hut over there," Sergio whispers.

"Wait, that hut!" Maria Beppina says, recognizing it. "This is the clearing where we stopped. This is *our* fire!"

"But how could it have come back alive?" Sergio says. "Primo kicked dirt on it."

They walk out from behind the tree to examine the situation, and that's when they hear something—a noise—coming from inside the shepherd's hut.

Snoring!

Maria Beppina's eyes go wide and so do Sergio's. Someone *is* here! Whoever it is, though, Maria Beppina and Sergio will never know.

They are already running home.

TOC

TOC

7
CURIOSITY

TOC TOC

Maria Beppina is happy to hear Primo's knock. She's curious what happened at the Tree of the Janara the other night, as she hasn't seen him since. It's almost like he's been avoiding her, or maybe it's everyone. He didn't even come to dinner last night!

As soon as she opens the door, Primo says, "Take it." He's holding out his hand, and Maria Beppina can't believe what's in it.

It's the ring.

"What are you giving me *this* for?" she asks as Primo places the ring in her hand.

Primo peers inside the doorway to look at

Maria Beppina's father, who sits working at his drafting table. His tools always spook Primo. "I want you to ask *him* about it," he whispers, nodding over.

"My dad?" Maria Beppina says. "Why?"

"Because he can read *all* the books," Primo says, and starts back down the steps.

"Did the Janara ever come to your tree?" Maria Beppina calls after him.

"Just ask your father about the ring!" Primo hollers up without looking back.

"What's going on out there?" her father calls from inside.

Maria Beppina shows Daddy the ring and tells him how Primo found it inside of a fish. "What do you think it means?" she asks.

"It means nothing. It's trash," he says. "People throw trash in the river. Fish eat trash."

"But it's not trash!" Maria Beppina says. "It's a beautiful ring."

"Well, maybe someone threw it into the river on purpose then. Or it slipped off their finger while they were doing the wash. People lose things, you know."

Maria Beppina stays upstairs for dinner that night. She doesn't want to disappoint Primo with what her father said, and she barely feels like eating anyway.

Sitting in bed, she takes out the ring and holds it up to the bright moonlight. How pretty it is! She never noticed the pattern.

Then she notices something else—a symbol etched into the inner band. A hook, it looks like, or maybe it's a *J*. Could it be a clue to who it belongs to? A Janara?

In Benevento, curiosity is the most dangerous thing of all. Maria Beppina has survived here by *not* being curious, but she can no longer help herself.

Why did Mischief Season come so early? Did that eel really lead Primo to the Manalonga? What would happen if the Clopper caught a kid? Caught *her*?

And what about this ring? She slips it on her finger and holds it up again to the moon. It fits perfectly.

Is it truly magical? Would it really protect her against witches?

Maria Beppina has no earthly idea.

8

THE MOST AMAZING
THING YET!

"MARIA Beppina! Sergio!"

Maria Beppina hears voices calling from outside.

"Maria Beppina! Sergio!"

At the same moment Maria Beppina and Sergio open their shutters across the alley from each other. Below, the Twins are calling.

"We're heading to meet Primo at the watch-tower. We're going to play Storm-the-Castle!" Rosa calls up. "Do you guys wanna come?"

Storm-the-Castle! That's Maria Beppina's favorite game. She always plays the guard. Everyone else hates to, but she loves it.

On her way out the door, Maria Beppina

feels the ring on her finger. She still isn't sure what to say to Primo. But that hardly matters at the moment—what matters is that they are almost to the Theater!

Before she even knows it, the rest of them are off and running. She has even less hope than usual of catching up, and is stuck again in the repeating nightmare.

Rosa is so far ahead, and now Emilio! Sergio turns back for a moment to look at her, but even he is starting to pull away. And her shoe! It's about to fall off.

The sound of her heart thumping in her head is overwhelmed by the *clopclopclopping* behind her. This is it, this is the time she is going to get *caught*! What can she do? She takes a big breath in. And she stops.

She just stops!

Maria Beppina stands in the middle of the wide open Theater, alone. The sound of clopping gets louder for a few steps. Then the clopping stops.

There is now only the sound of her own heavy breathing. And someone else's. Maria Beppina takes her deepest breath . . .

. . . *and*
   turns
      around.

Maria Beppina stands face to face with the Clopper.

The Clopper is much shorter than she expected—only her own height—and Maria Beppina finds herself staring straight into her eyes. These eyes are blinking, foggy, and don't seem to see very well. Or maybe they just can't believe what they *do* see.

A long time passes—as long as the time between lightning flashing and thunder clapping.

Finally, the Clopper speaks.

The Clopper rubs her chin, looking like she's lost something. "I'm not sure," she says, and begins to walk toward the walls of the Theater. She stops and turns back.

"Well, aren't you coming?" the Clopper says, holding out her hand to Maria Beppina.

Maria Beppina looks across the Theater to her friends, trying to catch their breath. She could run. Just run and join them, and never worry about the Clopper again. She looks back at the Clopper's hand.

Maria Beppina decides to take it.

9

THE HOME OF THE CLOPPER

LEADING Maria Beppina to a partly buried arch of the Theater, the Clopper unlocks a rickety door of roughly nailed together boards. The passage is so low that even Maria Beppina has to duck to go through.

The Clopper leads Maria Beppina down a pitch-black set of stone stairs, her wooden shoe clopping louder than ever, echoing off the walls.

"What is your name, dear?" the Clopper says, pressing Maria Beppina's hand a little more tightly between her bony fingers.

"Maria Beppina," Maria Beppina says.

At the bottom of the steps, the Clopper lights a candle, revealing a secret world.

"Do you like chamomile tea, Maria Beppina?" the Clopper says, setting the candle to some twigs in the fire-place and hanging a kettle there.

Maria Beppina nods yes.

What happens next is odd. The Clopper sets a table with two normal-sized cups and three small ones. At once, a bat, an owl, and a rat emerge from the shadows to join them at table.

"These are my friends, Sigismondo, Bruno, and Rafaella," the Clopper says.

The three of them chatter and hoot, almost like they were talking in a real language.

"Are they *demons*?" Maria Beppina asks. The chattering and hooting stops. "Not to offend you!"

"Oh, they aren't offended, sweetie," the Clopper says, pouring them each some tea. The bat and rat each skillfully use their wings and front paws to put a lump of sugar in their cups, while Sigismondo the owl drops two in with his beak.

"Owls like their tea *very* sweet,"

the Clopper says. "And demons too."

"Do they know the black
rooster who lives in the alley behind the blacksmith's
house? He always attacks my
father," Maria Beppina says. "Daddy
is sure he's a demon."

"Well, why don't you ask them?"

Maria Beppina does, strange as it seems.
The animals confer with one another, gestur-
ing with their paws and wings and shrugging.
They shake their heads *no* to her.

Rafaella, the bat, squeaks something. "There
are so many demons here you can't know every
one of them," the Clopper says, translating.

"But don't you all meet around the Tree of
the Janara?"

At this, the three smallest guests laugh. Maria Beppina didn't know animals could laugh.

"I don't understand," she says.

"Oh, you don't need to, dear!" the Clopper says, patting her hand. "It is so *nice* to have a child come to visit!" she says. "Can I get you something to eat, dear?"

"Sure," Maria Beppina says.

The Clopper moves around, looking in old pots and crocks, but can't find anything. The rat, Bruno, helpfully scurries down from his perch into a hole in the wall and comes back holding a half-eaten cookie in his mouth. He lays it in front of Maria Beppina.

Maria Beppina smiles, politely pretending to nibble on it.

"I'm sure I had food *some*where," the Clopper says, clopping around with her one wooden clog.

"What happened to your other shoe?" Maria Beppina asks.

"My other shoe?" The Clopper looks down, surprised to see one of her feet is bare.

"That's strange. Where *is* my other shoe?"

The animals all chitter and hoot and laugh again.

"Do you have any brothers or sisters, dear?" the Clopper asks.

"No," Maria Beppina says. "My mom died after she had me."

"Oh, I'm so sorry, sweetie," the Clopper says. The animals look down into their cups of tea, also sorrowful.

"It's okay," Maria Beppina says. "I mean, I never knew her. And it's kind of like I have brothers and sisters, because we live upstairs from my cousins. It's just, well, I'm not sure whether or not they *like* me."

"NONSENSE, dear!" the Clopper says. "How could *any*one not love you!"

The ceiling rumbles, and from the world above comes the sound of kids screaming as they run across the Theater. Maria Beppina points up. "Don't you have to do something about that?" she asks.

The Clopper looks puzzled.

"You know, *chase* them," Maria Beppina says.

"Oh, no," the Clopper says. "I hardly ever run after children anymore. They hear my footsteps even when I'm not there. They scare themselves." She chuckles into her teacup. The animals laugh too, and so does Maria Beppina.

Maria Beppina thinks about asking the Clopper why she started chasing after children

in the first place. There are *so* many things she wants to ask her about—the Janara, the Manalonga, the ring—but the Clopper is doing something better than answering questions. She's *listening.*

So Maria Beppina just talks to the Clopper. She talks about her father, and her downstairs neighbors, and her friends, but mostly just about herself. The Clopper laughs pleasantly at everything Maria Beppina says, and so do her demon friends.

Another pot of tea and many cubes of sugar later, the Clopper leads Maria Beppina back up the dark stairs. The door opens with a creak, the sun pours in, and the old witch blinks.

"So I guess this is what I do when I catch someone," she says to Maria Beppina, patting her hand. "I have them in for tea."

10

THE TALE OF MARIA BEPPINA

MARIA Beppina wanders home in a daze. She snaps out of it when she turns the corner and finds all the other kids gathered around the foot of her stairs. They seem to be waiting for someone. *Are they waiting for **me**?*

When they catch sight of Maria Beppina, the kids rush to surround and hug her.

"What happened? What happened?" they say again and again.

Maria Beppina is confused. It didn't occur to her that the others would think anything at all had happened to her. But they've been worried about her—really worried!

"What happened? What happened?" they keep repeating.

"It was . . ." Maria Beppina starts to say, but *what* is she going to say? Her first instinct is to lie—to say she was hiding in an arch of the Theater, or that she never tried to cross the Theater at all. But why would she *lie*? Maria Beppina hates to lie!

"It was the Clopper!" she blurts out. "She got me!"

"NO!"

"Wow!"

"Unreal!"

"How?"

Maria Beppina again wants to lie, and isn't sure why. She goes to say something, then doesn't, then starts to say something else, then doesn't again.

"I stopped!" she says at last, forcing herself to tell the truth.

"You stopped?" Rosa says.

"On purpose?" Emilio says.

"That's the bravest thing I ever heard of!" Sergio says.

"Why would you *stop*?" Primo asks.

"To see what happened," Maria Beppina says. "And what happened was ..."

Maria Beppina looks at the faces of her friends—they all want to be a part of her adventure. It makes her realize *why* she doesn't want to tell them the truth. Because if she does, then Primo and Rosa and Emilio will all want to go meet the Clopper and her

three demons. And if they do, then Sigismondo, Bruno, Rafaella, and the Clopper will become *their* friends too, and it will be about the other kids, like always, and not about her.

Maria Beppina wants to stay the only child the Clopper ever caught.

So Maria Beppina tells a fib.

"It was *terrible!*"

The wide-open eyes of her friends open *WIDER.* They want to hear more, and Maria Beppina's fib turns into a giant, whopping **lie**.

"The Clopper grabbed me and dragged me down to her underground lair! And then she locked me in a rusty cage and started a fire under a giant pot. There were three hideous demons helping her and they were all starving hungry! They talked this crazy language that I couldn't understand, but I could tell they were going to boil me!"

Maria Beppina has hardly ever lied in her life, but once she starts, it feels good. And the more the other kids hang on her every word, the more it gets her to telling **bigger** lies.

The words are no longer in her control— it's like someone else is telling the story, and Maria Beppina is watching it happen in front of her eyes.

The epic struggle of the wicked Clopper and her minions against the heroic girl. The girl who dared to stop!

"The Clopper kept laughing this horrible laugh and calling me *dearie* and *sweetie* and telling me how nice it was to have a child to eat after all these years," Maria Beppina says.

"This is amazing!" Emilio says.

"*Amazing!*" Sergio says.

"It's not just amazing," Rosa says. "It's the MOST AMAZING THING THAT EVER HAPPENED!"

Maria Beppina basks in the glow of amazingness. Then comes the question: "How did you *escape*?"

How did I escape? Maria Beppina wonders. *How **did** I escape?*

All at once the words stop flowing, and the more Maria Beppina tries to think about how she escaped, the more she can't think of what to make up. How exactly can a girl locked in a cage escape from a vile witch and her three vicious demons just as they are about to boil and eat her?

The *real* trap she's in, Maria Beppina realizes, is her lie!

"It was the ring!" Primo shouts. "Don't you guys see? The ring *protected* her from the Clopper!"

"Is it true?" the other kids say.

All eyes turn on Maria Beppina. What should she say? She can stop lying and tell them the truth and go back to being the same old Maria Beppina everyone ignores. Or she can say what she does say.

"Yes. Yes, it *is* true. The ring even started to glow."

The other kids get even *more* caught up in the tale, and Maria Beppina keeps going.

The ring, she says, blinded and seemed almost to burn the Clopper, so much so that the witch opened the cage and begged Maria Beppina to take the ring far away from her.

"I actually felt kind of bad for her as I left," Maria Beppina says.

And so the tale of Maria Beppina and the Clopper ends. Everyone loves it! Everyone is thrilled!

Everyone, that is, except Primo.

What happens next happens so suddenly Maria Beppina isn't even sure what is going on.

All at once, no one is listening to her. Instead, they are all following Primo—herself, the Twins, Sergio, and even Isidora—as he marches them all the way through the city gate to the foot of the bridge that leads to the Twins' farm.

"The ring," Primo says to Maria Beppina. "Give me the *ring*!"

She twists the ring off her finger and hands it over without a word.

Then Primo tells them his plan. "I'm going to walk up the bridge and I'm going to *stay* on the bridge," he says. "And I'm going to *talk* to a Manalonga."

"Don't be stupid, little brother!" Isidora says, but Primo is already walking up the ramp of the bridge. All the other kids yell at him to come back.

*This is **all** my fault!* Maria Beppina thinks. It was the lies—her lies! Her story convinced Primo that the ring *is* as magical as he thought, because it protected her from the Clopper. But the Clopper is just nice! And now if Primo gets snatched, it will be because of her!

"Primo, no!" she yells, joining in a chorus with the other kids. But it is all happening so fast!

Already at the peak of the bridge, Primo

takes one step toward the edge, and another.

"Primo! It's not true!" Maria Beppina yells. "The whole story was a—"

Maria Beppina never gets to finish her sentence.

She is being struck by something—some-thing falling from the sky. Isidora grabs Primo and pulls him down the bridge. As they run back toward town, Maria Beppina slips and falls on her butt. There are balls of ice everywhere, and now more and more, hitting her in the head, rolling down the bridge. It's a hail storm!

She slips again getting up, and the other kids are far ahead of her, running into the old

watchtower in the city walls to take cover.

Maria Beppina comes last, as usual, although she hardly cares. She's just relieved that nothing had happened to Primo! She can't believe he actually went to *talk* with a Manalonga! That's the bravest thing she's ever *heard* of!

Maria Beppina arrives in the watchtower to hear the echo of a loud slap, and sees Primo rubbing his red face and Isidora yelling at him for being so stupid.

"If bravery equaled smarts," Emilio says, "then you'd be a genius."

"Bravery *is* genius," Maria Beppina says, throwing her arms around her cousin. "And so are you, Primo!"

She's not even sure what she's saying or what it means—at the moment, she would defend Primo against anything or anybody in the whole world. She's just so happy he's alive!

Everyone has to yell over the sound of the hail hitting the stone tower, but everyone would probably have been yelling anyway.

All the attention is back on Primo, and Maria Beppina is relieved. And happy, for once, to be a little bit invisible.

11
PARTY TIME

"YOUR dad is *always* doing something fun," Maria Beppina says to Isidora.

The two cousins are sweeping up the downstairs, which is empty. All the furniture has been moved out into the street to make way for the dancing.

Uncle Mimì has hired a band of musicians to come play at the house tonight. Everyone is excited. (Well, everyone except Aunt Zufia.) Nonna Jovanna in particular loves a party and has been singing old songs all day.

"Girls, come and help me with the food!" she happily calls Isidora and Maria Beppina.

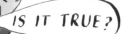

IS IT TRUE?

As they cut vegetables for the soup, Maria Beppina's dad comes in.

"Is it true?" he says. "Is there really a band of musicians from *Naples* coming here tonight?"

Daddy loves music, but he loves Naples even more. He always talks about moving back there, and whenever anyone from Naples comes to Benevento he corners them and talks their ear off.

While the adults speak, Isidora takes a rest from chopping, and moves some limp hair out from in front of her eyes. Her face is pale. She hasn't seemed well for days—since the hail storm, basically.

"Are you okay, Isidora?" Maria Beppina asks.

"Yeah, yeah, I'm okay," she says, like she got caught doing something she didn't want anyone to see. She quickly goes back to chopping. "How about you?" Isidora looks sideways at Maria Beppina. "How are *you* feeling?"

"Fine," Maria Beppina says, surprised by the question. "Why?"

"Well, after your terrifying escape from the Clopper, I'd expect you to be exhausted!" Isidora says with a big smile on her face.

Embarrassed and afraid of getting caught in her lies, Maria Beppina stares down at the carrot she's chopping and doesn't say anything.

Isidora looks like she feels bad for what she said. She moves closer to Maria Beppina.

"All the witches aren't as harmless as the Clopper, you know," Isidora says quietly. "Be careful."

*How does Isidora **know** the Clopper is harmless?* Maria Beppina wonders. But she isn't going to ask—Maria Beppina just wants the conversation to end. She is too afraid of her lie being found out, because then what would the other kids think of her? What would *Primo* think of her?

It has been an all-new Primo the last few days. He actually seems *happy* to have Maria Beppina living upstairs. For the first time, she feels like a part of the family.

The band starts to play, and Primo's poppa pulls his momma into the center to dance, and even Aunt Zufia can't help but enjoy herself. Maria Beppina likes watching everyone do the tarantella, but she definitely doesn't want to try it herself. She has no choice, however, when Uncle Mimì pulls her into the middle. She dances with Emilio, doing the best she can to copy what she's seen, and then Primo grabs her and *he* starts doing the tarantella with her.

Now it's just the two of them dancing, with everyone else clapping and stomping along. Primo smiles. He leans into her

ear and yells, "You're the brave one, cousin, not me!"

Maria Beppina feels herself blush. Tears well up.

"I'm not the brave one!" she wants to tell him. *"I'm a liar! And you could have been dragged down to the Underworld because of me!"*

Maria Beppina opens her mouth, about to tell him all of this—and more!—when Uncle Mimì cuts between them and grabs Maria Beppina's hands.

"My turn, niece!"

he says, pushing Primo out of the way.

As soon as she can get away, Maria Beppina heads outside, where she finds the others. With the Janara mischiefs finally over at their farm, the Twins are in a mood to celebrate. Sergio, on the other hand, is not.

"My problems are **NEVER** over," he says, pointing up to his ghost's apartment. Then, to what looks like an empty window, Sergio shouts, "I know, I know, but what am I supposed to do about it?"

Sergio turns to the others. "He's complaining about the party," he says, meaning the ghost. He puts his hands over his ears. "I hate it when Bis-Bis yells at me like this."

No one else, however, can hear a thing.

Sergio trudges up the stairs to talk to his ghost, and everyone says good night.

"What did you want to tell me back there?" Primo asks Maria Beppina as she climbs the stairs to her apartment.

"Oh, I forget," she says, and slips inside.

Maria Beppina goes to bed, but sleep is impossible. The party is still going on downstairs, with music and loud laughing and stomping feet. And then there's all the noise in her head.

Should she have told Primo the truth? Or is it okay to lie when you are keeping a secret?

There are other things to wonder about too. Like: What made it hail? How is it that Primo *didn't* get snatched by a Manalonga there on the bridge? Could he be right about the ring? What if it *was* the reason the Clopper and her demons were nice to her? The experience with them seems so strange now, Maria Beppina starts to wonder if it really happened at all.

The curiosity gets Maria Beppina up out of bed. She puts on her dress and goes down the stairs. Nearing the Theater, she happens upon Amerigo Pegleg. With his eyes closed, the old soldier dances to the distant music, spinning himself around on his wooden leg like a top.

Now, Maria Beppina stands at the edge of the open arena. She grew up with Daddy telling her how the Romans used to feed prisoners to the lions, and how the people in the audience cheered. When she came here, she always felt like one of those prisoners. Not anymore.

She starts walking. Not running, but *walking*. Slowly. Her heart thumps, but there is no other sound, no clopping.

Maria Beppina arrives at the short rickety door that leads down to the Clopper's.

Should she knock?

Yes. Because beyond fear, beyond curiosity, there is something more important. She wants to see the Clopper and the three demons again because they are her friends, and she wants to tell them all that's happened. They'll think it's funny, won't they?

She knocks.

TOC TOC

"Is that you, dearie?" Maria Beppina hears a muffled old lady voice from somewhere deep inside, as well as hooting and chattering. "Oh, let me open that for you! I can make you some chamomile tea...."

Life goes on, but our book is done!

So now you you know who we three really are. HELLO! You have also witnessed that curiosity is not such a bad thing after all, and certainly more important than always following the rules.

And what of YOUR curiosity, dear reader? Do you wonder about the same things that keep Maria Beppina awake at night? Or other questions, like who was sleeping in that hut? Or what that mark on the ring really means? Or how Isidora knows the Clopper is harmless?

I could tell you, but isn't it
more fun to find out on your own?
Read on, dear friend, read on.

Sigismondo
RAFAELLA
BRUNO

S.   R.   B.

WITCHONARY

IN Benevento, any kind of supernatural being is called a witch. And boy, are there a *lot* of them.

The Clopper: An old witch believed to be the last of her particular kind. She haunts the open square of the Theater, chasing children who dare cross it. Every kid in Benevento knows the *clop clop clop* of her one wooden clog!

Demons: Wily magical creatures who live among humans disguised as animals. In Benevento, 1 in 7 cats are demons, unless they are black, in which case it's 2 out of 3. Dogs, on the other hand, are never demons. Goats almost always are.

Ghosts: Spirits of those who died before their time. They must be taken care of by the descendants in whose homes they dwell. (Also called Ancestor Spirits.)

Goblins: Animal-like creatures whom Janara often keep as pets.

Janara: (Juh-NAHR-uh) Certain men and women can transform themselves into this type of witch by rubbing a magic oil into their armpits and saying a spell, after which they fly off to their famous tree to start a night of mischiefs. Janara belong to a secret society and don't dare reveal their secret identities to anyone!

Manalonga: (Man-uh-LONG-uh) The most feared of all witches. They lurk under bridges or inside wells and try to snatch children for un-known (but surely sinister) purposes.

Mares: A type of goblin who sits on children's chests at night, causing bad dreams.

Spirits: Witches who have no earthly bodies and live in one particular place, be it a house, chim-ney, stream, or arch. Types of spirits include ghosts, house fairies, and water sprites.

Life was very different in
Benevento in the 1820s.

HERE'S HOW THEY LIVED.

❖ Could kids read? No way! Not many of
them, anyway. Their parents couldn't
read either. Reading was considered
weird.

❖ Eyeglasses were rare. Since folks couldn't
read anyway, there wasn't much point.

❖ Shoes were only for fancy people.

❖ Forks were considered fancy, too.
Why use utensils when you can
use your fingers? Especially for
pasta! (Which was then called *maccheroni*.)

❖ Most people spent a lot of time hungry,
especially in winter. All food was local,
so you could only eat what was in
season, or preserved somehow. There

was no canned food, no refrigerators or freezer. Come February, people ate a lot of dried beans and figs.

✧ Stairs were on the outside of houses, even if the same family lived on two floors.

✧ Most people never lived anywhere but the home they were born in. Some never left the town they were born in. Not even once.

✧ There was no electricity. For light, you used a candle or an oil lamp.

✧ Houses didn't have water, either. To get some, you needed to take a bucket to a well or fountain. To wash clothes, you went to the river. Oh, and if you needed to use a toilet, you had to go outside for that, too!

If you want to learn MORE, please visit www.witchesofbenevento.com.

HISTORICAL NOTE

THE WITCHES OF BENEVENTO is set in 1820s Benevento.

Benevento was an important crossroads in Roman times and was the capital of the Lombards in Southern Italy during the early Middle Ages.

Even before the Romans conquered it, the town was famous as a center of witches. (Its original name, Maleventum—"bad event"—was switched by the Romans to Beneventum—"good event"—in hope of changing things. It didn't work.) For hundreds of years, Benevento was believed to be the place where all the witches of the world gathered, attending their peculiar festivals at a walnut tree near the Sabato River.

The people of Benevento, however, never believed there was anything wrong with witches, and maybe that's why they had—or thought they had—so many of them.

JOHN BEMELMANS MARCIANO

I grew up on a farm taking care of animals. We had one spectacularly nice chicken, the Missus, who lived in a stall with an ancient horse named Gilligan, and one rooster, Leon, who pecked our heads on our way home from school. Leon, I have no doubt, was a demon. Presently I take care of two cats, one dog, and a daughter.

SOPHIE BLACKALL

I've illustrated many books for children, including the Ivy and Bean series. I drew the pictures in this book using ink made from black olives and goat spit. This year, I received a shiny gold Caldecott Medal for *Finding Winnie*. I grew up in Australia, but now my boyfriend and I live in Brooklyn with a cat who never moves and a bunch of children who come and go like the wind.

Read all the books in the
WITCHES of BENEVENTO
series!

MISCHIEF SEASON:
A Twins Story

Emilio and Rosa are tired of all the nasty tricks the
Janara are playing when they ride at night making
mischiefs. Maybe the fortune-teller Zia Pia
will know how to stop the witches.

THE ALL-POWERFUL RING:
A Primo Story

Primo wants to prove he is the bravest, but will the
ring really protect him from all danger—even from
the Manalonga, who hide in wells and under bridges?

Coming Soon!
RESPECT YOUR GHOSTS:
A Sergio Story

Sergio is in charge of Bis-Bis, the ancestor spirit who
lives upstairs. Unfortunately, it's hard to satisfy all of the
ghost's demands and still keep Sergio's mother happy.